5/00  JJ

# Jan Ormerod
# MIDNIGHT PILLOW FIGHT

CANDLEWICK PRESS
CAMBRIDGE, MASSACHUSETTS

Have *you* ever woken up in the middle of the night?

Have *you* ever had a midnight pillow fight?          Polly has . . .

and look how it started.

Polly thought her pillow was alive.

She thought it wanted to play.

Has *your* pillow ever wanted to play in the middle of the night?

Polly's has.

Look, they went downstairs on tiptoe.

Polly peeked and what did she see?

For a moment Polly stood
and watched.

Some cushions were awake too.

I wonder what she felt, don't you?

This is how Polly said hello.

And this is how they played.

Now where did these big cushions come from?

Have *you* ever marched and danced like this,

having lots of fun in the middle of the night?

Look, they played leapfrog. Up and over . . . up and over . . .

up and over!

BUMP!

Oh, poor pillow!

Polly pushed – would *you* do that?

Polly got ready to fight.

Ready, steady . . . WHOOSH!

WALLOP! WHOOSH! WHOP!

WHOOSH! WHOP! WALLOP! *"Please stop!"* Polly turned on the light.

And the pillow fight stopped.

Polly put the cushions

back in their places.

Everything was still again.

Polly took her pillow up to bed.

Why do you think she looked so sad?

Have *you* ever hugged your pillow in the middle of the night? Polly has.

And look! All the cushions came upstairs to see if Polly was all right.

Have *you* ever woken up in the middle of the night? Have *you* ever

had a midnight pillow fight?  Polly has. . . and this is how it ended.